Deadly Incision

RORI BLEU

ROSIE CHAPEL

First printing: 2024
ISBN: 978-1-7635407-5-0 (eBook)
ISBN: 978-1-7635407-6-7 (Paperback)

Ulfire Pty. Ltd.
P.O. Box 1481
South Perth
WA 6951
Australia

www.rosiechapel.com

Cover Design: Rosie Chapel

Images sourced from Canva and Pixabay (courtesy - fszalai) using
appropriate licences.

Deadly Incision

Rori Bleu
Rosie Chapel

<h1 style="text-align:center">Chapter One</h1>

4th April 1888

"Hear ye, hear ye. Read all about it! Victim of vicious attack in Whitechapel, dies in London Hospital. Read all about it," the high-pitched proclamation of the young newsie peeled from Hyde Park Corner.

"I'll take a paper," Mr Philip Eaton, newly appointed head of the surgery department at the very same hospital, called to the lad.

"That'll be tuppence, sir."

Eaton dug in his pockets to discover he only had a thruppence and a sixpence to his name. The latter was required to pay for a hackney to the hospital, but the thrupenny bit could be spared for the paper and boy. Besides, he felt magnanimous dispensing worthy coin to lesser mortals.

"Make sure you do not squander the change, boy, and get your family a loaf on the way home."

The good doctor liked to exude an air of munificence in

front of the urchins who trolled the city streets in search of handouts.

The newsie looked at the coin and chuntered under his breath about the parsimony of the fancy dressed man.

"What was that you said, my lad?"

Barbarous lot these scum, Eaton thought to himself as he waited for the boy to explain himself and hand over the paper. The city ought to appropriate some of the treasury to the expansion of the workhouses. At least they would put these vagrants to good use.

"I said, thank you, sir," holding out the paper, the boy lied through his teeth. "I know me ma'll be cheered by yer charity, sir."

In truth, the boy had not seen hide nor hair of his parents in the two years since they abandoned him at a market in the East End.

Convinced the boy had insulted him, however obliquely, Eaton snatched the paper and used it to deliver a sharp whack to the boy's head, chiding, "Best curb that tongue around your betters, boy, and be thankful I did not choose to remove it instead."

The sun was peeking over the horizon, the faint brightening of the sky heralding the parade of lamplighters like moths to the flickering flames they were about to extinguish.

While he did not have to justify his actions to so lowly a station, Eaton was glad none of them witnessed him castigating a foul-mouthed child. It was beneath him.

The boy's punishment dispensed, Eaton made his way toward the hospital.

The click-clacking cadence of the brass heel of his cane against the cobblestones, echoing in the early morning air, marked Eaton's sudden exit.

His head smarting, the newsie's snivelling threats followed Eaton down the street. "If I see yer 'round here agin, yer'll be carrying that fancy stick up yer bloomin' arse."

Once on the main thoroughfare, Eaton waved down a hansom. Giving the driver the address, he climbed aboard, and made himself comfortable in preparation for the ride to the London Hospital in Whitechapel.

Eaton detested rubbing shoulders with the dregs of society but his position, as the youngest chief of surgery at any of the city's hospitals, meant this was a necessity. To his relief, although a burden he had to grin and bear, such contact was minimal. Regrettably, even his status as third son of an earl, did not open doors to the finer medical institutions.

Ah, his dear old father. The man never missed an opportunity to demonstrate his displeasure at his son's refusal to follow tradition by choosing medicine over the church. To abandon God for a secular position had left his father uncharacteristically speechless, although he knew better than to stand in Philip's way, hoping the rebellious streak might wane.

To this day, every morning as Eaton got ready for work, he heard the earl's voice in his head, decrying his son's poor choice of occupation with ritual frequency, inevitably concluding with… "For the love of God, man, you would serve Queen and Country better as a butcher. Why, why did you not enter the priesthood?"

Alone in his hackney, he found peace and solitude, if only briefly.

Snapping his paper open, Eaton leant against the window to allow the morning sunlight to illuminate his news of London. He searched the paper carefully, for the particular article with which the newsie had hawked his wares.

Amid ads for corsets and men's beaver skin top hats, Eaton found the story.

Emma Elizabeth Smith of 18 George Street, Spitalfields, London, fell victim to a brutal assault at the junction of Osborn Street and Brick Lane, Whitechapel in the early hours of Tuesday the 3rd.

Conscious when she was brought to the doors of London Hospital, she slipped into a coma and passed unto the Good Lord's care the next morning.

Her assailant or assailants remain unknown because Miss Smith refused to divulge their identities before succumbing to her wounds.

Eaton skimmed through the remains of the report. It offered no details regarding the extent of the woman's injuries, but noted an official inquest would be held within the next few days.

Eaton was irritated that no one from his hospital had seen fit to contact him about this case, although, the illustrious Mr Benjamin Hillier's name tagged as the surgeon on duty was sufficient explanation for the oversight.

Doubtless, the aging doctor would use the fact, the attack had occurred overnight on Easter Bank Holiday for not bothering the surgery chief with the menial case. Arguably, Benjamin Hillier bore a grudge against the younger doctor who had been conferred the appointment Hillier expected to have bestowed on him by right.

Ten years Eaton's senior, Hillier had done little to distinguish himself from those, Eaton considered to be common Whitechapel quacks littering the side streets, and he used what he perceived to be Hillier's inadequacies to stifle the withered doctor's chances of promotion, entertained by the latter's obvious acrimony.

Chalking up the omission as another example of Hillier's passive-aggressive nature; a psychological shortcoming, which, along with his failure to cultivate beneficial connections, had prevented Hillier from advancing in the profession. His pitiful attempt at vengeance by presenting Mr Eaton as an absent and negligent attendee, reduced to nothing more than a childish outburst.

"I will schedule a conversation with the good doctor," Eaton told the broadsheet.

Eaton's office mimicked those of his fellow chiefs of surgery located across the city. One wall dedicated its life to a makeshift medical library. Among the books, several, penned by John Hunter, dated back to the eighteenth century and the dawn of modern medicine, as well as a sixteenth century treatise from, arguably, the father of modern anatomy, Andreas Vesalius.

To his right, a large window overlooked the bustling street outside the hospital, opposite of which was displayed an oversized etching of the hospital the day it opened, nearly a century and a half ago.

On the wall behind his desk, in pride of place, his diploma in pre-clinical medicine from Cambridge and his diploma for surgery from the College of Surgeons. He always took a moment to admire his achievements.

Hanging his topcoat neatly on his coat rack, the chief surgeon set the stack of files on his shabby desk, which had aged as poorly as the hospital in which it was housed. His chair creaked its daily resentment of the doctor's use, prompting Eaton to gripe, "One day, you wooden fussbudget, I shall end your ceaseless complaining and toss you into a bonfire."

Finding the sweet spot where his chair was silent enough

to allow him to proceed with his tasks, he read through the first set of documents.

It was an account of the corpses the hospital had in storage currently. With the addition of the recently deceased Emma Smith, there was a grand total of two mouldering in his morgue's icehouse.

"Unacceptable," he grumbled. "How can a respectable hospital, such as the London, continue to train surgeons without the proper resources?"

A cursory review of the morning paper had divulged the story of a single execution at Newgate Prison. Eaton jotted a note to send one of his men to collect the body before scroungers from Saint Mary's Hospital beat him to the cadaver.

"This daily competition is becoming ludicrous," he lamented. "If only our beloved Queen had not listened to her long dead husband.

Grave robbing, among the world's oldest professions, had come into its own during the last two centuries when countries across Europe granted permission for cadavers to be used for the purposes of medical study.

Since Prince Albert's death from typhoid and exhaustion, Victoria had spent her years, and a substantial amount of the country's wealth, in mourning.

Eaton's suspicion that the Queen was losing her senses was exacerbated when someone from Windsor Castle leaked the particulars of a recurring dream which troubled the monarch.

According to sources… unnamed, obviously… her adored husband visited her night after night to plead for the protection of the dead laid to rest in London's cemeteries. He feared for the safety of those who could not defend themselves, which meant maintaining guard over the graves.

As per Albert's wishes, Victoria had ordered the

Metropolitan Police to increase their presence and patrols around the cemeteries, especially those housing fresh burials.

The monarch badgered both Houses of Parliament to stiffen the penalties for anyone caught robbing graves, declaring that protracted incarceration in Reading Gaol was the only acceptable sentence. Her hope... the silence and isolation endured by the prisoners, would act as a reminder of the mortification suffered by the departed six feet under.

Due to these ridiculous measures, the cost of suitable corpses had soared.

Eaton began to read Hillier's autopsy report which included crude sketches of the victim's body.

Infuriated at the almost illegible penmanship, he threw the sheets on the desk. "I don't know what is more atrocious, his lack of surgical skill or his handwriting."

His aggravation exacerbated by the suspicion, the old man had probably destroyed any organs the hospital might have used for instruction.

Determined to see the extent of butchery inflicted on his cadaver, Eaton rose from his chair, ignoring its groan of protest, and marched briskly to the surgery ward.

Chapter Two

Eaton stopped at the nurse's desk in the corridor. He had scant time for women as a whole, let alone women in medicine. He married for no other reason than social etiquette dictated it; his well-concealed reluctance tempered, fortuitously, because his wife brought a substantial dowry to the union.

"Miss Thompson," gruffly, Eaton addressed the nurse in charge of the ground floor. "Please summon the orderlies and dispatch them to Newgate prison to retrieve the body from yesterday's execution, before it disappears or is dumped in a pauper's grave."

Eying the brash surgeon, Miss Thompson considered giving him a thorough tongue-lashing. She had better things to do than play housemaid for this lobcock but, to protest might lead to her dismissal for the day without pay, or worse — a charge of insubordination for refusing to assist a bloody doctor, followed, in short measure, by termination of her employment.

Damping down her abhorrence, Miss Thompson placed her fountain pen on the tray next to its matching inkwell, carefully, so as not to stab him with it, nor waste her expensive ink tossing the glass well at his head.

She mustered up a bland smile. "By all means, Mister Eaton, I shall see to it immediately. Is there anything else with which I may assist you…" she could not hold her tongue, "…whilst in the midst of completing my reports?"

Eaton paid no heed to her cynicism, choosing to assign her another task.

"How generous the offer, Miss Thompson. If you happen to see Mister Hillier, please let him know I am looking for him."

Deciding not to press her luck, Miss Thompson waited for the windbag to finish speaking, then informed him politely, "You will find Mister Hillier in the operating theatre. I believe he is preparing for his lecture on the murder victim."

"A butcher describing a butchered corpse. That should be charming." Eaton turned on his heel in disgust and left without a word of thanks to the nurse for her help.

Eaton strolled into the operating theatre to find Mr Hillier preparing for his lecture. The ascending rows of wooden benches, reserved for the aspiring young surgeons, remained empty. Barring interruption owing to an emergency aside, class was not scheduled to begin for another forty minutes.

He stood in the hallowed hall and took a deep breath. This was the domain of erudite men, and it pleased him to know women would never taint this sanctuary of medical learning. Not if he had any say in the matter.

The aroma of varnished wood and formaldehyde, teased

Eaton's nostrils. The sunlight through the widows and the glow given off by the softly hissing gas lamps, did not quite dispel the slightly macabre ambience which came with the awareness this was where death lurked.

Hearing footsteps, Hillier glanced across to see the young usurper. "Ah, Mister Eaton. To what do I owe the honour of your presence? Does a floor need mopping, or mayhap one of the toilets is blocked?"

"My dear Mister Hillier, your mockery cuts me to the quick. I thought to take the opportunity to revel in your vast anatomical knowledge. Surely you would not deprive me of your expertise."

"Those words dripping from your lips sound like clap-trap. I will allow you to attend my lecture if you promise to behave."

"You have my word, Mister Hillier." Eaton pledged as he moved to an empty perch in the corner.

The room filled with scholars looking to prove their lot in life. Of the twenty-five attendees, Eaton judged approximately three would get to practice inside a reputable hospital.

Most would see their skills squandered in some back-street clinic or employed to amputate legs in the Queen's military. Two, he decided condescendingly, would be better served attending the races at Kempton Park.

Once the students had settled in their seats, chatting amongst themselves, a couple of orderlies lugged a large blackboard to the 'head' end of the operating table.

Rapping his wooden pointer on the aging board, Hillier admonished, "Gentlemen, silence please. If I may have your attention. We have much to cover today."

Pinned to the blackboard, four photographs of the

recently departed Emma Smith. One was of her poor bludgeoned face... probably taken prior to her death. Begrudgingly, Eaton credited Hillier for his foresight. Hopefully taken *after* he realised he could not save her life.

The second picture was a close up of the cut to her ear.

The third was an image, even Eaton found disturbing. It was a post-mortem photograph of the deceased's vaginal area. A blunt instrument, presumably the same weapon used to beat her almost to death, had been inserted with brutal force.

According to the haphazard note Hillier had left his Chief Surgeon, the object had ruptured Smith's peritoneum, leading to her death.

While the picture disgusted Eaton's genteel English upbringing, it refused to loosen its grip on his attention.

The final picture was a body-length photograph of the naked corpse, as well as a sketch of her head indicating where she was struck.

Leaning back against the bench, Eaton made a mental note to have a conversation with the old man about using hospital funds unnecessarily. Mentally, he totted up the cost of hiring an outside photographer, dry plates, and no doubt — given the quality of the photographs — platinum paper.

Make sure to deduct the amount from the good doctor's pay.

"Gentleman," Hillier began. "Allow me to introduce Emma Elizabeth Smith, age undetermined. Occupation, prostitute. Can any of you hazard her cause of death?"

Artlessly, but with a hint of schoolboy petulance, Eaton let slip his displeasure for Hillier. "Her attending physician?"

The class rocked with mirth, quashed when Hillier brought his pointer down onto the table with a loud thwack.

"Mister Eaton," Hillier chastised. "If you cannot be a

constructive member of this discussion, I must ask you to leave."

"Please excuse my ill-mannered comment and, if I may, owing to the grievous trauma to her vagina, I daresay she died of peritonitis. Unlikely to be caused by over-zealous customers. As for the injuries to her head, while vicious in nature, they did not contribute to her death. If I was to essay a reason for the attack, I postulate this began as robbery perpetrated by one of our colourful East end gangs, which escalated to rape and led to her death."

Hillier chuckled, "Gentleman, despite rumours to the contrary, it seems Mister Eaton can indeed read my reports. Let that be a lesson to you. Note taking is not a pointless exercise. When we are called to the bar, especially in a murder case, concise recollections can mean the difference between a man's freedom and the hangman's noose on the Newgate gallows."

The remainder of the class covered the adverse effects of peritonitis on the female body and showed examples of how quickly it had contaminated Miss Smith's organs.

He called upon various students to identify a specific organ preserved in formaldehyde and how the illness might have affected it.

As the lecture drew to a close, notwithstanding his opinion of the man as a surgeon, Eaton had gained a kernel of respect for Hillier's abilities as a teacher. Still, the doctor needed to be reminded of his place.

Eaton joined Hillier who was gathering his equipment. Picking up the specimen jar containing Smith's stomach, Eaton commented, "That was quite the lesson you presented, Mister Hillier."

Slightly taken aback at the long overdue compliment from his superior, Hillier stuttered, "T-Thank you, sir."

That was when the Chief Surgeon dropped the other shoe on Hillier's ego.

"Next time, do not expend hospital resources without consulting me first. Never mind that we have to find something in our already tight budget for the extra ice we shall require to preserve the various cadavers until the exam, photographic paper and the services of a trained photographer do not come cheaply. Money we cannot recoup given, even if she had family, it is unlikely they would spend a farthing to claim her body."

Confused by the speed with which Eaton shifted from complimentary to critical, Hillier took refuge in the defensive, "Mister Eaton, had you cared to be at work any earlier, you would have been as repulsed by the stench as I. You cannot expect these gentlemen to be subjected to effluvium compounds."

"Hillier, let me remind you, you are training the next generation of surgeons. The aroma of death should be one they become accustomed to as quickly as possible. If they cannot control the contents of their stomachs or their ability to remain conscious, I suggest you see they find their way to other occupations.

"Perhaps recommend your students smear a drop of camphor under their nose. Apparently, the Americans are experimenting with a compound of that and menthol. Although, they are chasing a cold remedy of all things. I digress. Have you given any more thought to our conversation about these gentlemen's final exams?"

"Yes, and again I express my disquiet about expecting the students to acquire their own cadavers. Queen Victoria must understand the importance of anatomical research, and the lack of viable candidates. She has to recognise our needs as a teaching hospital?"

"Do you wish to debate that with our Queen… or better yet… Prince Albert. I'll wager she might not appreciate your presence in her chambers waiting for his chimera to manifest."

"It is worrisome all the same. To force them to purchase bodies, recalls Frankenstein and his Monster, and what of those who cannot afford to do so?"

"As to your first concern, Mister Hillier, the hospital is not granting permission for these future men of science to go digging up bodies in the local graveyard. There are more lucrative markets for obtaining such."

"For those who are but an economic breath away from quitting. What do we tell them?"

Eaton brushed a bit of dander from the old man's black wool jacket. "Inform them, as with their fellow students, they will be expected to obtain a cadaver, no exceptions."

He turned, leaving Hillier standing aghast at the unspoken innuendo.

Chapter Three

6 August 1888

A protracted heatwave had resulted in the wealthier students securing their required cadavers. The easy coin offered to families whose elderly relatives had succumbed to the extreme summer temperatures to be escorted by Death to paradise, meant the necessity to scrounge up money they did not have for a decent burial was no longer a problem.

Regrettably, the less fortunate in the class, faced the probability of failing anatomy because of lack of resources. A dilemma which brought Thomas Fairchild to Mr Eaton's office.

The young man fidgeted nervously in the chair across from the Chief Surgeon, waiting for Mr Eaton to address him.

Eaton shut the ledger containing the school's accounting for each student, as well as the resources each had managed to procure.

Setting his steel pen on the tray next to the inkwell, his

eyes flitted to Fairchild. Taking his spectacles from the bridge of his nose, Eaton settled back in his chair, which squealed a protest.

"Mister Fairchild," although well aware of the reason the would-be surgeon was in his office, social norms applied, "to what do I owe this visit?"

"M-mister Eaton," the young man stammered. "M-my family is dealing with some financial… difficulties. My mother has taken ill and is confined to bed, and my father's agricultural investments have fallen short of expectations. I fear I cannot procure a cadaver for our finals."

The chair legs grated on the floor when Eaton rose. He crossed to the window and stared out onto the hustle and bustle of London's East End.

"Are you aware of the number of nameless and faceless immigrants who call Whitechapel home?" he asked. "Some thirty thousand, whose lives are anything but irreproachable, especially at night. I should hate to dismiss you, my boy, for lacking the forethought to handle your problems yourself."

Eaton paused his rebuke as two women passing beneath the window caught his eye, *doubtless heading to the local taverns to begin their nightly prowls,* he thought scornfully.

"What do you suggest, Mister Eaton?" Fairchild's question broke into his rumination.

"Dear Lord, Fairchild, I should not have to spell it out. The sun is setting, yet here you are, sitting on your sorry backside in my office. Now, go."

Eaton watched Fairchild scramble from his chair and leg it, hoping the idiot had decoded his message. There was no way he could, overtly, instruct the boy to go out into the streets and take a life. That was a crime the hospital would not tolerate. Nor would the city authorities condone culling the herd even if it was for the betterment of the overcrowded population of the poor.

Pondering whether the would-be surgeon was worth the bother, Eaton shrugged, gathered his coat and hat, and called it a day.

6 August 1888
Before Midnight

Fairchild had spent the better part of the evening patrolling the local taverns on the mission to which he assumed the Chief Surgeon had alluded. Dissatisfied with the quality of potential cadavers he had encountered holding up the bars in previous establishments, he happened upon the Angel and Crown public house.

The taproom was crowded, most patrons drunk beyond reason.

He ordered an ale and supped it, considering whether to call it a night, which he judged a fool's errand, go home, and prepare for whatever penalty Mr Eaton deemed appropriate.

Until he heard the banter bouncing back and forth between two women and two men. The latter, given their uniform, Fairchild assumed to be soldiers, while the women were obviously prostitutes.

He observed the quartet while they drank, his attention fixed on the plumper of the two women.

I could overcome any resistance she might offer, Fairchild determined. He raked his gaze over her, assessing her health. The slight yellowing of her skin indicated she suffered from cirrhosis of the liver, owing to overindulgence of alcohol, rendering that organ useless. That aside, she appeared otherwise well fed and fit.

. . .

The woman in question, spotted the intensity of Fairchild's brooding gaze, and whispered to her friend, "Come on, Poll. Let's find some other place to enjoy ourselves."

"Whatevah for, Martha?" Mary Ann Connelly — better known as Pearly Poll to her friends, various barkeeps, and assorted *acquaintances* — quizzed. "It's warm in 'ere and these gents look like they 'ave more coin goin' a beggin'."

"Mebbe so, but I dun't like the way that bloke over there is staring at me. Gives me the creeps, it does."

"Yer a daft cow, Martha. 'E's too much of a toff to bother with the likes o' you. 'Ave a gander at 'is fancy clobber. 'E'll be one o' them wot likes to come down to Whitechapel to..." Poll feigned a snooty accent, "view the locals, like we're an h'exhibit at the bloody zoo."

"I dun't care wot you fink, Poll. There is sommat wrong wiv 'im."

"Fine, hush yer whining," Poll relented.

Poll smiled disarmingly at the two soldiers, "Me mate 'ere would like to invite the two o' yer to a better class o' party. Seems that geezer is making her skin crawl."

The two men glanced at Fairchild, who averted his gaze. The larger of the two growled, "Yer want me to knock his block off? I 'aven't 'ad a good scrap in a while."

His friend interjected, "Yer wanna spend the next three weeks confined to barracks?"

"They'll 'a' ter catch me first." He smirked. "'Is nibs ain't got no business coming dahn 'ere to gawk. 'E should be taught some manners."

Martha put her hand on his arm. "Let it lie, Archie. More fun to find a quiet spot for wot's left o' t'night."

Bowing, he smiled. "By all means, m'lady." Making Martha chuckle.

The four left the public house reeling together happily.

Fairchild gave them a few minutes head start before he followed. On the path, he paused, listening in an attempt to locate them.

To his good fortune — although hampered by people milling about in various stages of inebriation, and the pall of the Whitechapel night — he spotted of the foursome at the entrance to the alley connecting Wentworth and Whitechapel High Streets where they separated into two pairs. His target and her man turned down the lane, while the other couple continued on in search of their own dark recess.

Once the latter was out of sight, Fairchild crept to the corner to follow Martha. Hugging the walls of the alley, he stopped when he heard a heated conversation erupt between the prostitute and her *beau*.

"I dun't care 'ow much yer willin' ter pay, I ain't that type o' woman. In fact, you can take yer coins and shove 'em up yer bum."

"Well, lah-di-dah, yer a right bloody tease," the soldier snorted. "Anyway, yer owes me, after drinkin' 'arf me money. Mebbe it's you who needs to be taught a lesson in the Queen's manners."

The sound of a fist striking saggy flesh, then a shocked yelp, reached Fairchild as Martha berated, "Git yer arse away from me, afore I cuts yer again."

Fairchild heard the thud of heavy boots fading as one of the pair dashed down the alley… thankfully, in the opposite direction from where he loitered.

Calmly. Fairchild strolled towards the woman, taking care to see in which hand she held her knife.

Using his most soothing tone, he asked, "Are you injured,

miss? I know a thing or two about medicine. May I be of service?"

Martha spun about on her boot, prepared to proposition the kindly stranger who dared enter the dark passage to assist her.

"No, sir, tha's kind o' yer, I guarantee yer in—"

Her words froze on her lips. Jabbing her knife at Fairchild, Martha snarled, "You. What in the blazes do you want?"

A chuckle broke from Fairchild. "More than you know, dear lady."

Martha slashed the jagged blade at arm's length… she meant business.

Fairchild ducked and grabbed a slat from a broken wooden pallet. With all the strength he could muster, he swung wildly at her hand, dislodging the blade.

The pair gaped at each other before Martha pivoted on her heel and darted down the alley.

Tossing the crude, wooden cudgel aside, Fairchild spotted the blade. Snatching it from the filthy stone flags, he pursued the fleeing woman.

Martha made it to the far end of the tenements which comprised George Yard Buildings before Fairchild tackled her. She landed on the street with a thud, her overfed body cushioning her attacker from suffering the same fate.

Without hesitation, Martha shrugged him off her back and kicked furiously, the toes of her boots bruising his legs. Self-preservation turning her into a hellion.

Martha's jagged blade in his hand, Fairchild plunged it into her stomach, severing the celiac artery.

Desperately, Martha shrieked, "Murder," hoping someone would come to her rescue.

No one did.

Fairchild grabbed her hair and dragged her up a flight of

wooden stairs connecting the separate floors of the tenement house, to conceal the crime he was perpetrating from unwitting passers-by.

The battle intensified. Fairchild only made it to the first-floor landing but, once there, something inside him snapped. A red haze descended and, overtaken by blind fury, he struck with savage frenzy.

Thirty-nine times, the old blade tore at her body. Nothing was spared. He stabbed her in the throat nine times, to prevent her from uttering another scream.

He punctured her left lung five times, her right, twice. One stab to her heart, five to her liver, two in her spleen and, finally, six slashes to her stomach and groin.

Fairchild's attack was so brutal, the battered metal broke, obliging him to use his penknife to finish the job.

Panting like a dog, sweat rolling down his forehead and into his eyes, Fairchild pushed himself to his feet.

Sanity seeped back into the young man, as he registered realized the error of his aggression. Not a single organ was worth salvaging from the woman.

Worse, Fairchild heard footsteps and the soft murmur of voices; people were climbing the stairs, towards them.

Hauling the bloodied corpse further up the steps, the young man waited for discovery, exhaling a silent sigh of relief when the couple turned along the first-floor gallery, quickly followed by the soft snick of a door closing.

Not a moment too soon, as Fairchild lost his grip of the grisly mess. Martha's body slid back down to the landing, her dress bunched up around her thighs, exposing her lower body, giving the appearance, she was the victim of a sexual attack.

Abject fear drove Fairchild down the staircase, and into the night. He slowed his steps when he came across a constable busy questioning the soldier whom Fairchild recognised as Archie.

"State your business. Why are you abroad at this time of night? Up to no good, I'll be bound."

Ensuring the copper could not see his wound, Archie bleated, "I am waiting for me mate, sir. We need to get to the barracks a'fore we get in trouble."

"Archie? Where the hell are you?" a voice hailed from the murk.

"Ah, and there he is," Archie said, sending up a quick prayer of thanks under his breath for Burt's timing. "Ah'm 'ere Burt, conversing wiv this upstanding officer. We ought ter be making tracks. Did yer get done?"

"And then some," Burt grinned.

Archie turned his attention to the Bobby, asking, "If yer satisfied, officer, we free ter take off?"

"Yes, and don't let me catch you skulkin' around here again," the constable warned, sent the pair on their way, and continued with his patrol.

Fairchild waited until the trio disappeared, in their respective directions, before emerging from his hiding place.

With no other choice, he headed to the one person who he hoped would give him refuge and a plausible alibi… Mister Philip Eaton.

As for the rest of Whitechapel, no one reported seeing or hearing anything suspicious, with the exception of one woman who was woken by someone screaming **murder** but paid no attention. It was Whitechapel, after all.

One of the tenement dwellers stumbled over Martha's body, as he ascended the dimly lit staircase to his room. Exhausted from his long day as a hackney driver, and the time coming up three-thirty in the morning, he assumed her to be a vagrant sleeping off a binge on the steps.

Not bothering to check on her condition, he swore at her, "Move yer lazy arse somewhere else, woman. There be hard-working 'onest blokes livin' here."

It was not until just after dawn, when a dock worker discovered Martha's mutilated corpse on the stairs as he left for work. He fetched a constable… the same one who had stopped Archie just hours before.

Soon, the tenement was awash with coppers scouring the area for clues, as a local doctor, roused to attend the scene, performed an ad hoc autopsy in situ to determine the time of death.

The investigation into Martha Tabram, age 39, began.

Chapter Four

As this was playing out, Thomas Fairchild, panting from his headlong dash and trembling from shock, stood in front of the Eatons' shiny black front door.

Commissioned by one of Mrs. Eaton's ancestors in the early eighteenth century, the house was part of her dowry. Philip Eaton detested the draughty place almost as much as he detested his wife.

Olive Eaton was roused from a deep slumber by the drum of a fist on the front door. Presuming it was a drunk messing about, she ignored it, but when it got louder instead of abating, she shook her snoring husband.

"For the love of God, someone is trying to break down our door. Go down and do something about it."

"Let them be," Eaton grumbled. "Even if they do break in, they will discover it was a futile attempt, we have nothing worth stealing."

"Which could well result," Olive tried to reason with her drowsy husband, "in them coming upstairs to murder us out of principle."

.   .   .

"Mister Eaton, I need to see you," The shrill voice of a young man seemed to reverberate around their bedroom.

"Goodness, Philip, why is someone looking for you at this time of night?"

Yawning, and realising sleep was now impossible, Eaton swung his legs out of bed.

"Perhaps it is an emergency at the hospital?" Olive posited.

"It damn well better be or there will be the Devil to pay."

"Philip Eaton, watch your tongue!"

As he stood, his nightshirt billowed about his knees. Crossing to the small hearth which warmed their bedchamber, he grumbled under his breath, "Mayhap whoever is at the door will indeed murder me to free me from this misery." *Better yet, rid me of my harpy of a wife.*

Grabbing the iron poker from its stand, Eaton stood at the top of the stairs, and yelled, "Whoever you are, away with you. It is well past midnight and we do not receive visitors at this hour."

The admonishment did not stop the unwanted guest from his determination to rouse the neighbourhood.

He thumped on the door, and a familiar voice shouted through the paneling. "Mister Eaton, it is I, Thomas Fairchild. I went to a pub, found a... and did as you instructed..."

Fairchild heard the sound of rapidly descending bare feet.

The door swung open and before Eaton could speak, Fairchild repeated, "I went to the pub, and did as you instructed, but it went awry."

Eaton refuted gruffly, "I suggested no such thing."

This refusal of fact stunned Fairchild momentarily but, collecting chaotic thoughts, he attempted to pin blame on the Chief Surgeon. "You most certainly did. You inferred that Whitechapel was teeming with people no one would miss, and I ought to take matters into my own hands. I did and I need the protection of you and the Hospital because—"

"Silence, boy. I do not know what misconception you gleaned from my question, but I assure you it had nothing to do with creating your own corpse. Away with you."

Arguing his case, Fairchild snapped, "I beg to differ, Mister Eaton, that is exactly what you were suggesting and, if you will not help me, I shall have no alternative but to repeat your statement to the Metropolitan Police."

The men's attention swivelled to the staircase, when Olive, standing at the top, asked, "Who is it, dear?"

"One of my foolhardy students. Seems the boy gathered enough liquid courage to challenge his dismissal from the Hospital's Surgeon's programme. Go back to bed, love," an endearment he had never used on his wife before, earning a puzzled grimace.

While something she had dreamt he might say, given the circumstances, it had the opposite effect and left her felling hollow and rejected. Without a word, she retreated to their chamber and let the door swing closed with a solid bang.

Below, the two stood in awkward silence.

.   .   .

Eaton looked at Fairchild. Resignation drenched his words, "I have no idea what you have done, nor do I wish to know but, as one of my students, I will permit you to cool your heels in my outhouse until we straighten out this matter. You'll be obliged to share your accommodation with a mound of coal and wood, but 'tis only a temporary resting place.

"I cannot have you wandering this city blindly, causing more mayhem. Follow the passage to your left, then turn left again and wait for me at the back gate."

"May I ask two questions? First, why are you holding the poker as though about to attack me?"

Eaton glanced at the rod in his hand and chuckled. "My apologies." He lowered the brass fire tool but did not put it down.

"Second, should I not wait for you here? I could become disoriented in the dark and lose my way."

"Which would be a boon for me," Eaton snarked. "I prefer you not loiter in my foyer whilst I seek my robe, slippers, and key to the outhouse. 'Tis a simple enough instruction. If you wish for my assistance, do as I say. Elsewise, begone."

The young man nodded and stepped back into the night, turning in the direction he was instructed.

Wearily, Eaton climbed the stairs to retrieve his slippers and dressing gown from the bedchamber. Olive said not a word to her husband, feigning sleep.

Eaton returned to the ground floor, and walked through the house to the scullery where he lifted the chunky outhouse key from its hook on the wall.

The poker tucked under his arm discretely, he left the house and crossed the tiny, stone-flagged courtyard to the back gate where he found Fairchild pacing.

"Would it not be easier for me to stay in one of your rooms, sir?" The student was beginning to question the wisdom of his late-night call.

"What plausible excuse might I provide for your presence? This is the easiest option."

Eaton unlocked the outhouse and allowed Fairchild to precede him inside.

The young man pulled his handkerchief from his pocket and covered his nose and mouth. Coal dust hung thick in the air. He was glad the doctor had implied his confinement would be mere hours, he doubted he would survive any longer.

About to thank Eaton for his salvation, Fairchild's gratitude was foiled by a searing pain to the back of his head, accompanied by a brilliant white flash, pinpricks of light dancing in front of his eyes.

Fairchild dropped to his knees, a second blow slamming into his head. Desperately, he tried to fend off the blows, sensing his skull crumbling in on itself; shards of bone piercing his brain.

The third toppled him against the coal. Darkness overtook him, his life spark rushed from his body, along with the last of his breath.

Eaton was not content to leave Fairchild in this condition. The boy was too easily identifiable.

Like a man possessed, Eaton smote Fairchild with the poker, unnecessarily guaranteeing his demise then rolled the body over and repeated his assault on the young man's face until it was obliterated beyond recognition.

Covering the remains with coal, Eaton devised a scheme to have Olive out of the house as soon as the shops opened, allowing one of his men to retrieve the body and add it to the collection of cadavers in the morgue before her return.

Brushing excess dust from his hands, he closed and secured the door.

Retracing his steps into the scullery, Eaton undressed, and dropped his clothing — liberally splattered with blood and smeared with coal — piece by piece onto the fire.

Indulging in a cursory wash, he grabbed a blanket from the linen closet. Hugging it around himself, he trudged up the stairs to his bedchamber.

His wife was sitting up in bed waiting for him. She pinned him with a queer look.

"Philip Eaton, what in God's name are you up to?"

Heaving a well-placed sigh, he explained, "After I sent that annoying drunk on his way, I decided to stoke the fireplaces. He let the night's chill permeate the house because he refused to shut the door.

"Unfortunately, the coal scuttle was empty, meaning I needed to visit the outhouse. Well, one thing led to another, and before I knew it, I was face first in the coal and ruined my nightshirt.

"I apologise for the inconvenience, Olive, but I must beg you to purchase me a new set on the morrow."

Olive appeared exasperated, first with the goings-on of their uninvited guest, and now with her husband's foolish request. Nevertheless, she obliged him, giving him a proper sounding all the same.

"You had best have a care, Philip Eaton. Even if you are Chief of Surgery for London Hospital, we cannot afford to waste money buying you clothes each time you need to warm your rear end."

"Forgive me, Olive, I pledge to watch my step."

"See you do. Go on, you need a proper wash, by which I mean, actually ensuring the water comes into contact with your skin," she tutted. "You look like a coal whipper."

"Could you not picture me at the docks on the Thames unloading those ships?"

"I daresay husband but, right at this moment I prefer not to imagine such nonsense. Use soap, I want you clean before you come back to bed."

Home by noon to minimise the chance of being seen by any of her friends, Olive visited Philip's favourite tailor where she was persuaded into two new nightshirts, glad of the plain brown paper in which the items were wrapped.

It was occasions like this, she wished they could afford a manservant to undertake such personal tasks.

It did present her with an opportunity to overhear a titbit of gossip while waiting for her purchases to be packaged.

Two other women were discussing a grisly murder which had occurred in Whitechapel earlier that morning. One let slip that her husband was assigned to the investigation.

"From the ghastly details, I am certain, once he solves this case, his superiors will have no choice but to promote him to Chief Inspector, and then we can afford to move to a better part of town."

The policeman's garrulous wife mentioned the location of death, leading Olive to contemplate whether the body would end up at London Hospital under Philip's care… mayhap leading to particulars about which this woman had no idea.

Olive also gleaned that the murder took place around the same time as the disturbance at their front door.

A coincidence Olive discarded, blaming the insanity which took place in the streets on the moon.

Her stroll home took her past a tattered cart exiting her neighbourhood. Peddlers, she frowned wishing there was a way to ban them from their neatly kept streets.

"I'll suggest that to Philip," she noted to herself.

Mr Philip Eaton was enduring his own trying day. Glancing at his pocket watch, he noted it was close to noon, and his man had yet to return with Fairchild's body.

"You cannot trust those simpletons to accomplish the most basic of tasks. I should have seen to it myself," Eaton brooded just as Hillier entered the Chief Surgeon's office without knocking.

"Problem, Philip?" Hillier asked.

"Besides your lack of decorum in forgetting to knock, just the usual frustrations. To what do I owe this unannounced pleasure?"

"A query. Did you receive any communication from Thomas Fairchild regarding an absence?"

"I neglected to inform you when I arrived this morning. I dismissed young Mister Fairchild from the programme last afternoon."

Hillier was flabbergasted. "For what reason? His grades were more than sufficient for the programme."

"His finances were not," Eaton countered. "London Hospital is not running a charity. He knew when admitted that he would be expected to keep up with his payments, as well as his studies. Neither do I need your permission to execute my duties for the sake of this institution."

"Perhaps not, but in the future, I would appreciate notification of any dismissals of my—"

"The hospital's…"

"…students from the surgical programme."

"Duly noted, Mister Hillier. While we are on the subject of students, you may be interested to note, a cadaver has been gifted to the hospital. It should arrive this afternoon. I understand it was a victim of a heinous attack. Apparently, the brain and skull are beyond any educational benefit but, surprisingly, the internal organs are intact. See which of our remaining candidates can take advantage of this good luck."

"I repeat, Eaton, your cavalier attitude towards the dead will catch up with you, one day."

"Until it does, we have a body with which we can earn a few quid. Now, leave my office and attend to your duties."

Huffing his pique, Hillier stalked out, and banged the door shut.

Chapter Five

30 August 1888

The dissection training began at tables arranged neatly around the Surgical Theatre. Each body was covered with a clean white sheet, a toe tag identifying its owner.

Upon Mr Hillier's pronouncement, the sheets were stripped back, exposing cadavers in various stages of decomposition. The decay of each decelerated — to the abject relief of the respective students — by dint of being kept on ice from procurement, until required to be thawed for this exam, gradually and under strict hospital guidelines.

The majority were in reasonable condition, death occurring from heart attack, heat stroke, or some other natural cause.

A few had died as a result of disease or trauma inflicted by their fellow man.

The room came alive with the sound of clicking metal and muted conversations.

The only student without the necessary cadaver was

Benton Warren, compelling him to observe those better prepared.

Irritated, Warren, who had dissected small animals since he was a boy, believed himself capable of a far more professional job than any of the toffs he was watching.

Absorbing as much as possible, he took up position across from a student exhibiting, in Warren's opinion, questionable skills. Warren's lip curled at the tremor in the young man's hand as he performed a jagged Y-cut on his cadaver to open the body cavity.

Following the path of the scalpel as it sliced through the lifeless flesh, Warren noticed a peculiar birthmark on the body. It was a deep purple circle, about the size of a lead ball, slightly to the left of the sternum, resembling a flintlock wound to the heart.

Acknowledging there could be any number of people with a similar birthmark, Warren knew the owner of this one... Thomas Fairchild.

The two had been chums since childhood. Warren used to tease Thomas that he must have been shot in a duel in a previous life.

Warren scrutinised what was left of the face, searching for any additional identifying features, but it was beaten to a pulp. It was the odd strand of tawny-brown hair, not soaked in blood and matted to the corpse's skull in stiff clumps, which confirmed Warren's suspicions.

The last time he saw his roommate was nearly a month ago when both were summoned to Eaton's office after class.

Interviewed first, Warren had slunk off to their rooms, without waiting for Fairchild who never returned.

Rumour had it that Thomas was expelled because of excessive debt, a fate Warren faced also. The latter remained baffled as to why his friend did not apprise him of the decision or say goodbye. Neither had it sat well with him when the school arranged to have Thomas' belongings packed and shipped to his parents' home in Canterbury, without so much as a by your leave.

Grieved at discovering his friend was murdered, Warren knew the information would be invaluable in ensuring he did not lose his place on the course.

"Gentlemen," Hillier announced as the clock struck four, "we are finished for the day. Please return your specimens to storage.

"Mister Warren, do not forget to see Mister Eaton before you go."

"Yes, sir," Warren replied with newfound confidence.

Unlike Fairchild, Warren was unmoved by the Chief Surgeon's bombastic disposition.

While the doctor rambled on about Warren's burgeoning debt to London Hospital, and his inability to fulfil necessary requirements, culminating in his intention to dismiss Warren from the programme, Warren settled into his chair and crossed his legs nonchalantly.

Warren's composure rattled Eaton. He was accustomed to grown men all but urinating in fear, but the student in front of him seemed barely interested. Was he even listening?

"You do understand what I am telling you, Mister Warren? Failure to produce a body by week's end will precipitate your immediate expulsion and forfeiture of any payment already applied to your academic debt."

"Yes, Mister Eaton, I understand. I feel, however, you have a proposal to circumvent that travesty, perhaps under much the same terms offered to the recently deceased Thomas Fairchild?"

Momentarily stunned, Eaton bit out, "I beg your pardon?"

"Come now, sir." Warren rose from his chair and straightened his suit. "We both know the cadaver on table five is… was… my classmate and friend. I am not sure who beat the life out of him, but I daresay you do.

Without giving Eaton, a chance to defend himself, Warren continued, "Be that as it may, if you grant me the terms, I will not fail as Thomas did."

Eaton barked a humourless laugh to cover a sudden wariness. "I have no idea what you are insinuating, but I can tell you the same as I did Fairchild. With so many nameless and faceless immigrants who call the East End home, an enterprising fellow such as yourself ought to be able to find a way to honour his obligations in order to retain his position in this school."

"You want me to create one, Mister Eaton?"

"Are you as daft as Fairchild? I would never answer such an absurd question," Eaton replied scornfully. "What I'm telling you is you should be bright enough to figure out a solution."

Warren simply smiled and reassured Eaton, "I will not fail, sir."

"See that you do not, for this is your only chance."

30/31 August 1888

Mary Ann Nichols reeled along Whitechapel Road to the Frying Pan public house in Spitalfields.

She had spent the better part of the day trying to scrape together enough pennies to cover the cost of a bed in her usual boarding-house, instead of resorting to resting her head in a corner of Trafalgar Square.

Regrettably, Mary's desire for booze had overcome her desire for a less uncomfortable night's sleep… three times.

She had already been booted out into the darkness by the landlady, who caught her trying to sleep in the kitchen of the lodging house.

The woman showed Mary the door, berating, "I can smell alcohol all over you. Yer drank the coin yer supposed ter be 'andin' over fer yer bed, yer daft mare."

Stumbling into the pub, she spent the next ninety-minutes frittering away more coin on drink for a fourth time.

A soft chime marked the half hour.

Bleary eyed, Mary stared at the clock tucked into the alcove, attempting to comprehend its meaning.

The barman chuckled at the uncoordinated antics of the intoxicated woman. "Lass, if yer ain't got coin to swill, bugger off."

"Bah," Mary slurred, reeling slightly. "This piss yer call ale ain't worth me money…ev'n if I 'ad any."

"Off with yer then," the barman retorted.

Mary staggered into a couple of chairs as she left the Frying Pan, singing about her jolly bonnet.

Hit by the chill of the early morning air, she sobered up… marginally.

"Hmmm… mebbe's there's time ter scrounge up a coup'l o' pennies."

As Mary teetered down Osborn Street, she was spotted by her old roommate, Emily Holland. The two had shared a single bed over the past few months, until the former was kicked out.

Emily feared for her friend's life. She had searched high and low for Mary after being informed by the landlady that her rent would double because she no longer had a bed mate.

"Mary, this ain't no time of the night ter be on yer own. Come on 'ome," Emily coaxed.

Mary waved her off laughing. "Em'ly, yer the last one who can afford ter be charitable. I'll be fine on me own, sleepin' under protection of the Admiral."

Huffing a sigh, Emily gave up and trudged off towards her lodgings. Her room might be miserable but at least it was dry. She glanced back once, to see Mary going in the other direction.

She bit her lip, contemplating whether it was worth chasing after her friend to drag her back to the boarding house but, by the time she decided, Mary had turned the corner and was gone. Emily dithered, but the frigid air sent her scurrying home.

Heading back to Whitechapel Road, Mary made it as far as Buck's Row before careening into a well clad gentleman whose presence in the shadows... had she not been three-sheets to the wind... Mary might have questioned... as she scarpered.

"Well, 'ello, guvnor," she made a concerted effort to sound coherent. "Wot find's yer out at this time o' night?"

"Just taking the air," Warren, hoping to sound as though this was not his habit, instilled a note of shy invitation into his reply. "I have a couple of shillings taking up space in my pocket, and am feeling generous, if you're looking for company.

"Say no more, guvnor. I know a way o' puttin' yer money ter good use."

Warren grinned at her offer. The flickering flame of the

gas lantern reflected against his teeth. His hand slipped into the pocket of his cloak, as he responded, "I believe I do as well."

Mary's eyes widened when in place of the shillings, she expected to be given, she saw the glint of a massive blade. Her scream died in her throat as a hand clamped over her mouth. The pressure so intense, she could taste the coppery flavour of her blood oozing from her gums, her teeth literally being squeezed from her mouth.

Wriggling frantically to escape this madman's clutches, came to naught as the knife was plunged into her throat, spearing into her spine, severing her larynx in the process. Had she survived the attack, her pleas would have been impossible.

A second wound paralleled the first, ensuring Mary's demise.

Observing the life fade from the woman's eyes, a strange sensation overtook Benton.

That this woman's body would benefit his medical training was of minor importance compared with the rush of adrenaline which flowed through him at the realization he was a god. He possessed the power to end life quickly and efficiently.

As Mary's last breath bubbled over her lips, Benton relaxed his grip on her mouth. Snagging a handful of the woman's hair before she pitched forward onto the cobblestones, he thrust his blade into her abdomen, mutilating her internal organs.

Dropping her onto the damp, unforgiving street, Benton finished his handiwork with several more lacerations to her abdomen, and two vicious stabs wounds to her groin for added measure.

Cleaning his blade on the dead woman's bonnet, Warren

tucked his knife into his cloak, and sauntered off, whistling a jaunty tune.

An Hour Later

A certain Mr Charles Cross… carman… half asleep… was trudging to work along Buck's Row, when he spotted what he assumed to be rubbish discarded in the street, at the entrance to some stables.

He complained balefully at the heap, "No wonder thems who 'as money come dahn 'ere to gawk. No bugger bothers to keep this place clean."

He treated the pile to a second glance and an aggrieved kick, aghast to register the pile of debris was actually a body.

"Wot we got 'ere, then?" Without the aid of a lamp, it was difficult to determine what kind of body and, despite knowing it was not, Mr Cross prayed for it to be a large mutt, there were plenty scavenging around the docks. Holding his breath, he peered closer, then jerked back. It was a woman, lying on her back, clothes awry, her hand touching the gate of the stable entrance.

Warily, he scanned his surrounds… whoever done her in might be lurking. The curious hush which had settled on the street at his discovery was broken by the rattling of wheels. Mr Cross looked up to see a cart approaching.

Cross hailed the newcomer, "You. I say you there, stop and give me a hand."

"Wotcha got?" the second man called.

"A dead body. Leastways, I think so."

The second man climbed down from his cart to join

Cross. "Robert Paul," he introduced himself, absently, his gaze on the body.

"Charles Cross," Cross replied in a similarly distracted manner as the pair examined the woman who was staring blankly into the night sky.

Robert grunted, "Bah. Jus' another drunk. Hospital's dahn the street. Why dontcha lug 'er sorry arse there and let them deal wiv 'er."

Charles touched the woman's face, sensing a lingering warmth, while her cold hands spoke of death.

"I tell yer, she'm be dead."

"Wot d'yer want me to do abaht it? I 'av' ter get ter work."

"Same 'ere, but we can't leave 'er like this."

"Fine, let's get a constable to worry about her. I can't be late for work again."

In accord, the two men went in search of the bobby responsible for this beat.

Chapter Six

From the moment the gruesome remains were discovered by one of three constables, the bobbies were embroiled in a flurry of business.

While the two cartmen sought help, Constable John Neil happened upon poor Mary as he made his rounds. He was joined by his colleague, Jonas Mizen, alerted by Cross and Paul who had vanished into the night as soon as they had reported their discovery.

Shortly thereafter, a third constable by the name of John Thain appeared and was dispatched to fetch Doctor Llewellyn. Which he did… post haste.

Dr Llewellyn arrived and, somewhat churlishly — the result of his rude awakening — conducted a perfunctory assessment, and confirmed she was, indeed, dead. Closer examination revealed that the deceased's body and legs were still warm, in contrast with her hands and wrists which were cold.

"She's been dead less than an hour," he surmised.

Thain stared at him, his mind summoning up a timeline.

"Lawks, that means 'im what done 'er in coulda been nearby when she were found. Mebbe even watchin'."

"That is a distinct possibility, Constable." The doctor nodded absently and frowned. These deaths were more than a trifle unsettling, especially since the yet-to-be-solved murders had begun in West Ham around six years ago.

He rose to his feet, brushed the knees of his pants, and ignoring the rational portion of his brain telling him it was not the fault of the constables that he kept being called out… *mind, if they did their damn job and caught the depraved brute, the East End would be a safer place…* vented his irritation on the undeserving Constable Neil.

"Dammit, man. Even the drunks here in the East End could have pronounced her. I am going home where any respectable citizen of London should be at this time of night, and I do not expect to be troubled again unless you find something more important than this…" In spite of his frustration, Llewellyn's tone softened in a modicum of respect as he waved his hand at the body.

Constable Neil, a man who took his job seriously, was not prepared to let the doctor… exhausted or not… off the hook that easily. Couldn't let any Tom, Dick or Harry pronounce a death… there'd be hell to pay, if he shirked his duties.

Unwilling to vex the irascible medic further, he sought to placate, "Sir, beggin' your pardon, and I know yer the expert, but surely the lack of blood surrounding the body must be significant?"

Grudgingly, Llewellyn conceded, "That *is* puzzling. Barely half a pint has bled out. It is conceivable your killer may have some anatomical knowledge, understanding that once she was dead, any further injuries would not cause a haemorrhage."

He sighed wearily. "That said, I leave you to do your

work, to return to my bed. There is nothing I can do for this poor woman now. Please arrange for her to be removed to Old Montague Street Mortuary. I will conduct a post-mortem later. I bid you good morning."

Doctor Llewellyn strode away without a backwards glance.

Smarting from the dressing down, Constable Neil, nevertheless, forced it aside for the sake of the investigation, pulled on his professionalism like a cloak, and got on with the job at hand.

He asked PC Thain to arrange for the transport of the body adding, "Then call upon the good doctor, but maybe delay for twenty minutes or so. Apparently, the poor man needs his beauty sleep.

"As for the rest of you, I want this area and its residents checked thoroughly. Leave no stone unturned."

Which they did, repeating the same exhaustive investigation as had been undertaken following the murder of Martha Tabram nearly a month earlier…. to the displeasure of the neighbourhood.

Doors were pounded on along Buck's Row, rousing anyone not already up and preparing for work.

Interviews resulted in scant evidence. While a few people admitted to being awake during the relevant time period, nothing suspicious was reported. Not even the bobbies on patrol at that time could offer anything pertinent.

As dawn broke, the scene attracted the attention of the locals who, in turn, faced questioning from the Metropolitan Police.

Once the body was secure at the mortuary, Constable Neil, with unapologetic satisfaction it cannot be denied, summoned Dr Llewellyn again… barely forty-five minutes since the physician had dismissed himself… to perform a thorough autopsy.

The rest of the morning, and well into the afternoon, remained similarly chaotic, and the identity of the victim was not ascertained until later in the day.

While confusion and fear ran rampant among the residents of Whitechapel, the same could not be said for the young man sitting patiently outside Mr Eaton's office in London Hospital.

Pleased with his night's endeavour, the smile on Benton Warren's face appeared indelible and, every so often, his fingers brushed the sharp metal secreted within his cloak.

Hearing the steady tread of Eaton's boots and cane along the Hospital's corridor, Warren scrambled to his feet to greet him.

"Marvellous day is it not, Mister Eaton?"

Eaton scowled at the student as he unlocked his door. "Shut your mouth and get inside."

Not even Eaton's vexed tone wiped the smile from Warren's face.

The door had not closed behind the pair, when Eaton fulminated, "I assume that mess down the street was your doing?"

Warren puffed up his chest at Eaton's recognition. "Clean and efficient. Took me less than four minutes to carve her up—"

"Which was not what you were sent to do, and your current euphoria leaves me troubled about your medical future."

"Did you not ask for a cadaver to be delivered to this hospital?"

"You are as useless as your friend," Eaton groused. "Neither of you possesses the intelligence the good lord gave a goose. I did not intend for you to commit murder. God knows there are enough derelicts along Whitechapel's roads to negate the necessity of adding to them."

"So, I dabbled in some late-night anatomy. In the end, you have your body, do you not? I all but delivered her to your doorstep. Your reaction baffles me, Mister Eaton. There was no harm done," Warren lashed out.

"No harm…" Eaton spat. "*No harm?* Let me tell you exactly what harm you caused, boy. You carved up and dumped, as did Mister Fairchild, a woman on the streets of Whitechapel. Then you had the inanity to leave her less than one hundred and fifty yards from our venerable institution.

"If that was not dim-witted enough, you did the deed on a bobby's beat. Why did you not invite the Metropolitan Police to stand next to you and watch you eviscerate the poor woman? Would save the city a small fortune hunting for you.

"Finally… and more concerning with regard to your ineptitude… was her body delivered to our hospital for dissection and investigation? Hell, no," Eaton exploded, slamming his fist on his desk.

"Her body was taken to a private mortuary. What good does that do London Hospital, Mister Warren? Care to enlighten me?"

Warren was about to give Eaton an answer, at least one he thought logical, but Eaton cut him off.

"It was a rhetorical question, you dolt. There is no explanation you can offer to save you from expulsion."

To Eaton's bafflement, Benton Warren erupted in thunderous laughter.

"Mister Warren, I fail to see the humour in any of this."

"How can you *not*, Mister Eaton? We are both men of science and reason. Your audacious slander aside, I posit that permitting me to become a certified surgeon was not part of your plan, despite my recently demonstrated skill in both. I am also pondering whether you presume my fate will be the same as that of my friend Mr. Fairchild."

Before Eaton could answer, Warren responded for him, "I can assure you though, unlike he, I have no intention of occupying one of your morgue slabs for some knacker to chop me into bits so you can dispose of me."

A trickle of ice slunk down Eaton's spine, as Warren issued his not so veiled accusation.

His fingers slid into the shallow drawer in the centre of his desk to search for the pearl-handled letter opener his wife had gifted him for their last anniversary. It might not be large enough to ward off Warren should he decide to attack but was probably threatening enough to dissuade him in the first place.

Eaton breathed a soft sigh of relief as his fingers grazed over the dagger-like opener. Retrieving it, he placed it on the desk in plain view.

His voice held the slightest of tremors, "T-there's no need to return to the classroom. I reiterate, you are no longer welcome on the course."

Warren stood, straightened his jacket, and donned his bowler. "Then, we go our separate ways. Now I have experienced the power of taking a life, there is little your pitiful school can offer me academically. If you wish to witness my growth, I suggest you continue to read the Times. I would be disappointed if you missed certain…" his smile bordered on wolfish, "…reports."

Warren doffed his hat to Eaton, leaving one last caveat, "It might behove you to note that, should you feel moved to inform the Metropolitan Police of my identity, I doubt you will find the inside of a jail cell, or the cinch of a hangman's noose to your liking.

"I bid you a good day, Mister Eaton."

The door rattled open and, just as quickly closed, leaving the Chief Surgeon to dwell on the creation of the monster he had just witnessed.

Chapter Seven

As the days progressed, Eaton attempted to eradicate any trace of Thomas Fairchild and Benton Warren from his memory. As far as the surgeon was concerned, both men were nothing more than manifestations of stress caused by Queen Victoria's descent into decrepitude.

The programme was in its final months, and Mr Philip Eaton was determined that each student would succeed, even if Mr Hillier found his colleague's sudden participation unwanted and exasperating. A graduating class of capable surgeons would bring honour to London Hospital… and would not do their personal reputations any harm either.

With respect to the world beyond the hospital walls, Eaton treated it with the same healthy antipathy as he would a patient with the plague.

He was unaware of Annie Chapman's murder, on the 8th September, despite the fact the press ran exhaustive accounts of her mutilation, stating various organs had been removed from her body, and were left on her shoulder or missing altogether.

It took the double murders of Elizabeth Stride and Catherine Eddowes, on the last day of the month, to catapult Eaton out of his indifference.

Eaton was surprised when Olive insisted, they spend a quiet afternoon together indulging in tea and cakes, worried this abrupt matrimonial goodwill did not bode well.

Olive did not fail to furnish his dread.

Her gaze fixed on the front page of the paper, Olive noted, "Gracious me, there were two more horrifying murders near your hospital the night before last."

Philip responded with an idle, "Hmm? What are you muttering about?"

"Would you please pay attention, Philip Eaton. There are matters of greater importance than your bloody cricket scores."

Olive's cheeks flushed brilliant crimson as she uttered the expletive. *Heavens, but her husband could try the patience of a saint.*

"I am sorry, my dear." Philip swallowed an aggrieved sigh and set aside his half of the paper. "You have my full attention. What issue in particular do you deem troublesome?" his tone, vaguely condescending.

"These Whitechapel deaths. The Times reports two more women murdered by that Jack fellow last night."

"I doubt his name is Jack," Eaton contested. He had a pretty good theory as to the killer's identity but could never share his suspicions with anyone. "Assuredly, that is a name the newspapers invented. I would hazard more probably a Thomas or a Benton."

"Those are oddly specific names."

"I am only speculating, Olive."

"Be that as it may, I pray you take care on your travels to and from the hospital," Olive beseeched softly. "I wish your father would use his influence to secure you a position at a more suitable establishment."

"A thought you must banish from your head, woman. I refuse to beg him for any assistance," Eaton retorted. "I would rather face that lunatic's knife…" he jabbed a finger at the paper in Olive's hand.

"Philip, do not say such things." Olive was mortified at her husband's careless disregard for his own life.

As though Olive had not spoken, Eaton continued brusquely. "…than be indebted to my father."

"Thankfully, according to the Times, the populace of Whitechapel is banding together in vigilance committees to hunt this person down."

Eaton mocked, "More like vigilantes made up of a handful of drunks wandering around with pitchforks. I'll wager they will likely either injure themselves or murder some innocent passer-by before they apprehend the real killer.

"Efforts would be better spent pressuring the London Council to petition the Metropolitan Police to clear the riffraff from the district and expel the cursed prostitutes who roam the streets at night."

Nonplussed by her husband's callous attitude, Olive sputtered, "How could I have married such a heartless man?"

"I dare say it was preferable to being an old maid," Eaton countered acerbically.

In disgust, Olive tossed her section of the broadsheet onto the table. "Philip Eaton, you are a cad. Mark my words, one day, women in England will be on the same economical and legal footing as men, and when that day comes, I shall take great joy in expelling you from my house."

Eaton scoffed at the notion, snatched the paper Olive had discarded, and snapped it open to pages two and three, purposely avoiding the front page, to demonstrate he alone was the master of the manor and all items therein.

Furthermore, no mere woman would ever command him to do anything he had not already decided to do.

Olive glared daggers at her husband and swept out of the parlour, her umbrage palpable.

Glancing over the top of the paper, Eaton shook his head.

Waiting a few minutes to ascertain his wife was not about to reappear, Eaton turned the paper to read the story beneath the bold printed headlines on the front page.

The article wasted little ink in introduction before it delved into the gruesome details of the women's deaths, numbering the latest victims, three and four.

Both had suffered deep wounds to their throats. The similarities to Mary Ann Nichol's death were pronounced, and Eaton reasoned the same was probably true of the subsequent victim.

A constable, who wished to remain anonymous, stated, "It appears the assailant was disturbed while he was attacking Elizabeth Stride at Duffield's Yard, and compelled to flee. He made up for the interruption by carving up Catherine Eddowes like a Christmas goose, less than half a mile away in Mitre Square."

The crude account upset Eaton but was almost innocuous compared with what followed.

Approximately halfway through the story, he found a troubling statement from the journalist concerning the repellent reactions not only of the residents of the district, but also of London as a whole.

Short of festive, which is not the most laudable reaction given the circumstances, this writer is at a loss formulate a palatable description for the excitement which prevailed in Whitechapel and its immediate neighbourhood throughout yesterday.

From the time the first news of these fresh murders began to circulate, the streets of Whitechapel were filled with carriages and carts alike, until well past midnight, bringing people of all social standings, hoping to catch a glimpse of either victim.

"This is truly the demise of Western Civilization," Eaton lamented as he folded the paper and set it aside. "If only those idiots possessed the wit to know they are playing right into Warren's hands. This is the circus for which he hoped."

9 November 1888

October brought no more deaths in Whitechapel, save the usual drunken knife fight or street brawl.

Those on the streets held the belief that *Jack* deemed it imperative to leave owing to the presence of Howard Birmingham's Whitechapel Vigilance Committee and the number of false arrests they were accused of making. Anyone who did not fit the model of a proper English subject was apt to find themselves dragged to the Commercial Street Police Station.

As for Eaton, he hoped Warren had grown bored of the dregs of Whitechapel and moved on.

Putting it out of his mind, he made his way to the thoroughfare outside Hyde Park. Gone was the regular newsboy from whom he purchased his paper. After the confrontation between the two, it appeared the former had elected to hawk his papers further down the street.

Eaton grumbled, "All the better. We do not need his type in our neighbourhood."

He waved down a hackney. The driver pulled up alongside, asking politely, "Where to, guvnor?"

It was not Eaton who answered.

A man came up behind the cabbie's would-be fare, and wrapped his arm around the man, seemingly pushing Eaton into the hackney.

Without looking up, the man whom the driver later described as shabbily dressed, his bowler pulled low over his eyes, making identification difficult, said, "Thank'ee kindly. My friend 'ere got so drunk, 'e wandered off and I thought I'd lost 'im. 'E ain't got coin for a cab."

"Aye, guvnor, I see it all the time. Alcohol dun't suit everyone."

"It is rare to find an understanding sort as yerself, sir," the unkempt man replied. "Here." He tossed a shilling. The throw and catch, perfectly timed.

"Mayhap, you can take us up to the Tower Bridge construction site. It'll give 'im time to sober up, afore 'e 'as to face 'is wife. If yer know what I mean?"

"Aye, me missus'd raise hell if I turned up drunk as that one. Climb in, sir, and we will be on our way."

The man nodded and joined Eaton in the cab.

Already, the effects of the curare were setting in.

When Benton Warren appeared behind Eaton, he had rammed the ice pick — which he had hidden up his sleeve — coated with the paralytic, between Eaton's four and fifth ribs, puncturing the chief surgeon's left lung.

Being left-handed benefitted the former because his action was obscured.

Before Warren climbed into the hackney, Eaton felt his lung start to deflate, the mass refilling with air and blood.

Warren hefted Eaton from the floor of the cab and manhandled him into the seat to face his killer.

Eaton could make out Warren's toothy smile but not his face.

Warren's self-absorbed importance suffused the hackney. "I'm happy to see you are not struggling against your impending doom. We are among the relatively few who understand the speed with which curare pervades the body.

"I am curious as to which will kill you first, the poison or your deflated lung, although, quite frankly, it does not matter. What does is having you as a captive audience."

Eaton managed to cough, "W-Why? I kept your—"

"Agreed, Doctor Eaton. You kept my secret faithfully, but for how long, I cannot be certain. Let us say this is added assurance."

The cab rattled over the cobblestones, jarring the rapidly failing Eaton.

"By my computations, your last breath should be approaching quickly, so, allow me to conclude what I thought you would approve of... my latest masterpiece. In fact, it is what I consider my pièce de résistance.

"The vivisection of a beautiful young woman in Miller's Court.

"I admit negligence on my part for not asking her name but, in Whitechapel, no one tells the truth about such things and, I am sure, the Metropolitan Police will discover it soon enough.

"I can imagine the circus which will turn out when they find her," Warren chuckled softly at the thought.

On a soft sigh, Warren admitted, "I wish you had been

there as an accomplice. The accommodation was… interesting. She was kind enough to take me to her abode where we could work in peace.

"I did my darndest to keep her alive as long as possible. My skills, honed at London Hospital, would make you proud. Flesh expertly flayed, organs carefully removed and placed where the constables could recover them easily, save the one or two pieces I chose as souvenirs.

"I even took her eyes just to test my hand."

"Y-You're mad," Eaton rasped, then slumped in the seat and expired.

"Maybe so, my good Mister Eaton, but then again, aren't we all?"

Warren leant over to check for a pulse. Finding none, he taunted, "I was going to invite you to visit me in the city of Chicago, if you recuperate, sadly that seems improbable."

Tapping his cane on the roof of the hack, Warren instructed, "Driver, pull over."

Alighting, he flipped the cabbie one more shilling. "Make sure my friend makes it to the London Hospital. I fear he is not well."

From there, Warren vanished into the night.

The driver did as he was told, with alacrity.

At the hospital's doors, he jumped from his seat and hurried to check the passenger.

He found him dead, his mouth coated in white froth.

Bolting into the hospital, he shouted, "Please 'elp me. Me passenger's dead."

Mister Hillier, several orderlies on his heels, hastened to the hackney.

Hillier pronounced the man's death, exclaiming in shock, "My God, it's Philip Eaton."

Epilogue

London Hospital Morgue
One Week Later

In the time since Philip Eaton's murder, life had gone on without him.

Graciously, Mister Benjamin Hillier had accepted the post as London Hospital's Chief Surgeon. It came with extra responsibilities but, unlike his predecessor, he did not ignore his duties as an educator.

The late Mister Eaton's wife, Olive, put their house up for sale, claiming it held too many memories for her to remain.

Unbeknownst to those in her circle, she had decided to leave England once her finances were settled. She had heard Paris welcomed wealthy widows with open arms.

Prior to this, on a quiet morning in the morgue of London Hospital, Olive and Hillier stood next to an examining table where the body of Philip Eaton lay; a sheet draped over him.

Hillier glanced at the widow. "It is unusual to have you here. I beg you to keep this between us."

"Benjamin, for all you have done for me this past week, I could never do anything which might bring you shame or trouble. I simply ask to see my departed husband for the last time."

"You do understand a mortician has not been engaged to prepare the body for burial."

"Burial?" Olive replied, slightly amused.

Her tone perplexed Hillier. "Why, yes, I assumed you would want a viewing and burial for your husband. As is the custom."

"No, I daresay that would not be my dear husband's final wish, given his occupation."

Olive twitched the sheet to expose Eaton's lifeless face. She studied his features in silence.

Pursing her lips, she asked, "What does the medical school pay for a cadaver?"

The Meal

The Meal

William Carrington glanced at the clock, losing track of how many times he had already done so, satisfied, he still had plenty of time to finish dressing before his rented limousine appeared outside to transport him to his long awaited reservation.

Ah... the reservation, Carrington thought to himself. *Should I call again to verify it is indeed tonight and they are still holding a place for me?*

No... no, he relented, *the maître d sounded annoyed when I double checked earlier this afternoon. I must trust the table is there.*

Carrington had been planning this self-date for the last six months. He had scrimped and saved, religiously tithing to the fund created especially to pay for the meal in which he was preparing to participate.

He had driven his co-workers, at the *Bridgeton Brick and Masonry Depot,* to the brink of insanity with his constant descriptions of this night, of the food he anticipated tasting, and persistent requests as to the different options on the menu they thought worth trying.

The ringing of his doorbell informed him, his night was about to begin.

Rushing to leave, Carrington paused long enough to smooth even the smallest of wrinkles from his tuxedo, then swung open the door, to be greeted by a man in an equally immaculate black suit.

The man flashed Carrington a professional grin as he snapped a respectful bow.

"I will be your chauffeur for this evening," the driver informed his fare. "If you are ready, let us not tarry.."

The driver stepped to one side, to allow Carrington to pass, falling in behind as they strolled to the highly polished, black, 1954 Packard limo.

Both Carrington and limousine were products of a long ago era, compared with today's society but, to the man footing the bill for the evening, the match could not have been better.

He pictured himself as Cary Grant being whisked away to some movie release.

Before Carrington reached for the door handle, his chauffeur eased around him, nimbly, to open the door.

Sliding across the leather backseat, Carrington nodded to the driver as he closed the door behind him with a quiet click.

The pair made small talk while they drove through the quaint city nestled along New Jersey's Cohansey River, which drained into the Northern shore of the Delaware Bay.

While Carrington enjoyed the company, his attention lingered on the string of Victorian Houses lining the road. Behind the decorative facades of the whitewashed homes, they concealed a history of good times and bad; the city he had witnessed since his birth.

Most recently, Bridgeton had fallen victim to the loss of its manufacturing history.

Fortunately for Carrington, the owners of his company were determined to keep their brick and mortar plant an American company, instead of moving south with the remainder of Bridgeton's historic manufacturers and their related jobs.

Current history found a city rebounding thanks, in part, to an increase in crime across the state necessitating a new prison. Many who had found themselves previously unemployed, now patrolled the penitentiary's hallways.

Working in such a dreary setting was something Carrington had sworn never to do, even if it meant a significant pay raise.

Crossing into the newly renovated business district, he was happy to see the formally abandoned shops buzzing with activity... despite the fact, these businesses now catered, primarily, to the influx of nouveau-riche tech workers.

Coffee shops with their twenty-something hipster baristas, Carrington was sure he had heard that term used to describe them, dominated the sidewalks where, once, various Mom and Pop stores provided goods and services for the suburban families who lived in the small city.

At long last, the limo pulled to a squeaky, drum brake stop in front of an impressive restaurant. Flaming sconces flickered into the gathering gloom of nightfall.

Briskly, Carrington's driver circled the limo to open the door for his customer.

Alighting, Carrington smiled at the driver, who asked politely, "At what time shall I return to drive you home, sir?"

Leaning in to straighten the driver's tie, Carrington replied, "Why don't you take the rest of the night off and have some fun with your family."

"B-But, sir..." the driver began to object. "You have paid for the entire evening. I cannot shirk my responsibility to see you safely home."

Carrington had prepared himself for this argument.

"Do not worry, my friend. I have made arrangements for returning home."

Pulling two one-hundred dollar bills from his pocket, he stuffed them in the chauffeur's suit coat pocket.

"Buy a nice bottle of wine for your wife on your way home, as well as a proper chauffeur's hat for yourself. A uniform is not complete without the correct accessories."

Both men chuckled, then the driver said, "Thank you, sir. I hope you have an entertaining night."

"I can assure you, it will be eventful," Carrington replied before turning to the rather grand glass entrance.

The lilting tunes played by the three piece string ensemble gave the restaurant a European vibe.

Carrington paused next to the musicians, delighted by their rendition of Beethoven's Fourth Sympathy, Opus 60. It was one of Carrington's favorites and, because it was often overlooked by even the smallest of orchestras, it was akin to a hidden jewel.

As he listened, he scanned the patrons who had gathered for the first sitting, hearing their cheerful conversations. Mixed among enthusiastic family gatherings, several nervous-looking couples appeared to be on first dates, while others could be celebrating wedding anniversaries.

Carrington found the jovial atmosphere enveloping the room, soothing and welcoming.

Spying a man with a thin nose and even thinner moustache at the entrance to the dining room. Carrington assumed him to be the maître d'.

Carrying himself smartly over to the podium where the man stood, Carrington gave his name, "William Carrington," adding, "Esquire. I believe you have my reservation for a table for one," squinting at the man's name tag, "Reggie."

"That's Régis, sir"

"Excuse me?" Carrington asked in surprise.

"My name, sir, is Régis… not Reggie," the maître d' supplied, trying not to roll his eyes at the gauchely, over-dressed man.

"I do beg your pardon, Régis. Please forgive my error," embarrassed by his faux-pas, Carrington apologized profusely.

"Quoi que," came the man's terse reply. He assumed Carrington would not understand French, masking the fact he had written him off with a *whatever*.

Cynically, Régis smiled to himself at Carrington's simple, "Thank you."

Stupid Americans, he thought.

"What was your name again, sir?" he repeated.

"Carrington, William Carrington." Carrington thought it better to drop the Esquire this time.

"Oh, yes… Carrington." Régis ran a languid finger down the list of names, deliberately belaboring his search for the reservation; pretending not to see the numerous ticks against the diner's name, equating to how many times the latter had called to verify his booking.

"I see you requested a table near the window for the second session." Staring down his nose at Carrington, the maître d' continued, "Are you certain you would not be more comfortable nearer the back of the dining room? It is warmer there and the passersby will not gawk at you as you dine."

Carrington shook his head, "No, my good man, the table by the window is perfect."

"If you say so, sir."

Régis knew this man's appearance in the restaurant would discourage any foot traffic, once they saw him seated. "If this was my establishment, these imposters would never be allowed across the threshold," he grumbled under his breath.

"What was that?" Carrington missed the condescending comment.

"If you take a seat in the lounge, I shall see you are seated once your table is ready."

"Will it be much longer?" Carrington asked wistfully, wishing he had been able to reserve a first session instead.

"No, sir. We are readying for the change of service in a few moments."

Happy with the news, Carrington made his way to the finely appointed lounge.

Entering the darker room, he noted the walls were panelled in stained, red cherry. The huge mirror behind the bottles of expensive-looking alcohol reflected and refracted the muted incandescent light which glowed above them.

Taking a seat at the matching cherry-wood bar, Carrington waved to the bartender.

The snappily dressed man was finishing his customary performance for two young scantily dressed women, who were fascinated by his dexterity when flipping the alcohol bottles and the sterling silver shaker.

He filled their glasses, then tipped them a nod, as they applauded his skill, and stuffed tips in his jar.

He caught sight of the old man at the end of the bar, judging him to be a lightweight and a cheap tipper.

Stifling a sigh, he excused himself from the giggling women, summoned up a fake smile, and greeted his new customer, "Good evening, sir. How may I be of service?"

"My fine man, how about a gin martini?"

The bartender grimaced internally. The current consensus in the bartending world was that martinis should be created with vodka… not gin, which was decreed outdated for such a refined drink.

He also dreaded the next line, he knew was coming.

"Please make sure it is shaken, *not* stirred."

The bartender's smile never wavered and knowing James Bond's preference for vodka martinis over gin, replied, "Yes, sir. I promise a drink fit for an international spy."

"Please, do not blow my cover," Carrington chuckled.

"I would never consider committing such a travesty."

It took the bartender a minute or so to whip up the drink, forgoing any show he might have given anyone else.

"Would you like to start a tab, sir."

Taking a sip, Carrington shook his head. "No, this drink is more than sufficient… and quite tasty."

He tossed a fifty on the bar for an eighteen dollar drink, "Keep the change."

The bartender felt a twinge of guilt for misjudging his patron, which did not stop him from pocketing the change. "Thank you, sir."

Régis entered the lounge, and made a beeline for Carrington. Interpreting the reason, the bartender smiled at the elderly gentleman. "Your table is ready, sir. I hope you have a pleasant evening."

In a stiff and formal manner, Régis led Carrington to the window. Pulling the chair out for the guest, the maître d' sniffed as he scooched the seat back in.

Way too much aftershave and hair tonic.

"Your waiter will be with you in a moment to take your order."

"Before you go, may I ask a favour?"

"Is it something your waiter can handle? I ought to return to my station. Other guests are arriving and I must see to their needs as well."

A glance to the front by Carrington confirmed the legitimacy of Régis' excuse. "Yes, I do apologize for detaining you. I shall ask my waiter."

Carrington's waiter did not appear immediately. In fact, Carrington sat unattended for nigh on half an hour.

Still, he did not become upset.

He busied himself watching the evening traffic through the window, making up stories about where the occupants of the vehicles might be going.

When he grew tired of that, he observed the other diners around the room, and the various delicacies being served at their tables. He closed his eyes imagining the taste of their meals, knowing none would compare with what he had planned to eat.

Eventually, a young waiter appeared and introduced himself, "Good evening, sir, my name is Adam, and I will be your waiter this evening."

He rattled off a trite apology for the delay, then asked, "Are you ready to order?"

Carrington apprised the waiter, surmising he was barely old enough to work in an establishment which served alcohol.

No doubt a college student.

Without opening his menu, Carrington replied, "I would like the King's Feast."

The waiter paused, his pen hovering above the pad. "The King's Feast? Sir, are you sure about that? It's a lot of food."

"Oh, I am aware. You should find two *blue* lobsters reserved for me in the kitchen. I should like them brought to my table in a tank, so I may dine with them. Then I would like the chef to cook them for me table side."

"Ah… I need to check with management about that, sir."

"Please do so. I spoke to a very helpful, older lady. I believe her name was Roche…"

Carrington made it a policy to remember the names of those with whom he had made arrangements.

"…she might be the manager or the owner. I cannot recall which."

He knew full well she was the restaurant's owner.

"Anyway, she assured me when I placed the order, that it

would not be a problem since I prepaid the $1000 for the pair of them."

"Y-yes, sir." In a quandary, Adam looked back and forth between the diner and the maître d's stand.

"Go on." Carrington smiled. "I'm not going anywhere."

The waiter hurried across the room to Régis.

Hearing his name, Régis wanted to vanish into thin air, realizing from which table Adam approached.

In a hushed tone, he groused to the waiter, "Jesus Christ, why is he still not served?"

"We got busy… and I kinda overlooked him."

"Imbécile," Régis chastised.

Feeling the eyes of an elderly couple, who had just arrived, skewer him with disapproval, the maître d' reined in his annoyance.

Taking the young man aside, he asked calmly, "What's the matter?"

Glancing at the man, watching the pair from his table, Adam blurted out, "He has ordered the King's Feast."

"What?" Régis thought his ears deceived him.

The King's Feast was a twelve course meal, which took the entire sitting to prepare and serve, and comprised enough food for five people. That, and its cost, made it prohibitive for anyone to actually order.

It was on the menu as more of a joke, than a meal choice. The only thing it missed was a novelty T-shirt printed with some claim of surviving the gluttonous feast.

"Did you explain the meal to him?"

Lying to cover his ass, Adam said, "Yes, in detail."

"Well, as long as he knows, place the order. Just keep an eye on him, though. If he walks out without paying, you'll be footing the bill."

The waiter shifted awkwardly.

"Is there something else?" Régis's patience was on the brink of running out.

"Those two special order lobsters, Madame Roche had shipped in, are his and he wants them carted to his table."

The maître d' pondered the cost of the order.

As though a lightbulb had exploded in his head, he came to a startling conclusion, "Shit! He must be a food critic. Why else would he order, essentially, everything on the menu?

"Madame will have our heads for how he has been treated so far. Get your ass into the kitchen to start his order. Oh, and send the sommelier to his table with a bottle of our best house wine. Tell James to ensure our friend over there never sees the bottom of his wine goblet."

"Yes, sir." Adam sped off to the kitchen.

Seating the older couple and excusing himself, Régis appeared at Carrington's table.

The sommelier was already there, trying to convince Carrington, the Sauvignon Blanc, he was attempting to fill a glass with, would go perfect with his meal, even as Carrington was trying to refuse politely.

It was not that Carrington disliked wine, regardless of quality, it was more that he saw it as an unexpected, and unnecessary, cost.

Smiling obsequiously, Régis took the bottle from James and excused him.

"My apologies, Mr. Carrington. I neglected to tell James this bottle is on the house, with our compliments for purchasing such an exquisite meal."

With a delighted smile, Carrington relented and removed his hand to allow Régis to pour.

The glass half-filled, Carrington gave it a gentle swirl, allowing it to breathe, then took a sip.

"Very pleasant." He beamed his approval, and replaced the glass on the table.

Seeing the sous-chef pushing a cart with the tank of water containing the two rare, blue lobsters to the table, Adam in tow bearing a tray of goose liver hors d'oeuvres… signalling the commencement of the Feast… the maître d stepped out of the way.

Before returning to his duties, he added, "If you need anything else…" reassuring his, now distinguished, guest, "…please do not hesitate to ask."

Returning to his podium, Régis kept a sharp eye on the *critic's* table.

The night progressed quietly for the diners and staff of the restaurant. To Régis' delight, food left the kitchen in an expeditious manner, with no complaints.

He hoped the critic near the window took note of the efficient service.

Oddly fascinated, Régis watched the man consume his polenta cake with jam dead goat cheese as part of his amuse-bouche course, then advance to the third course with its Tuscan white bean and roasted garlic soup.

The waiter brought Carrington the fourth course appetizer of candied carrots with honey, cumin, and paprika.

After which, the guest seemed to savor his Greek salad with olives, lettuce, red onions, and feta cheese.

Régis was amazed the older man could stomach such copious quantities of rich food, finding the fact, Carrington was so slender, despite his occupation, slightly unsettling. Most food critics he had encountered were products of their gourmet lifestyles. This man might be a harsher judge when it came to the main courses.

The feast moved onto the fish course. Régis saw Maurice, the chef, leave the kitchen with a large pot of water and a cast-iron single burner.

The chef and the man at the table had a brief conversation where a disagreement occurred and Carrington appeared to dispatch Maurice back to the kitchen.

As the chef paused to push the door open, he gave the maître d' a Gallic shrug, indicating to Régis, he believed Carrington insane, then disappeared into the kitchen.

Excusing himself from guests who had arrived without reservations, hoping for an open table, Régis crossed to Carrington's table.

Reaching the diner, he noted the bottle of wine was empty, and motioned to James to bring another.

Courteously, he asked, "I-Is there an issue with the lobsters, sir. I could not help but notice you sent the chef away."

The answer was put on hold as the waiter arrived carrying the first main course; deep-fried turkey with a honey bourbon glaze. There was silence until the waiter had completed his task, and excused himself.

Carrington smiled cordially. "On the contrary. I am savouring every moment. Kudos to your staff."

"I am confused, sir. For the price you paid for the lobsters, why did you choose not to eat them prior to the meat course? Are they not to your liking?"

Carrington chuckled, "Oh gracious, yes. I could not ask for two more perfect specimens. I prefer, however, to treat them as a special dessert."

"I see… I think."

"In fact, I would be honoured if both you and the chef would join me to partake in them."

"Oh, sir, while they look delicious, regrettably, we have other guests whom we cannot neglect."

"I tell you what," Carrington proposed, never one to back away from a negotiation, "if my friends here are at my table by the end of the evening, the two of you will indeed join me."

Régis chuckled, "You drive a hard bargain, sir. Allow me to say, we shall see."

Carrington smiled. "I shall take that as a yes."

One eye on his odd guest, Régis noticed he did not take a single bite of the turkey. Concerned it was not to the man's liking, a frown marred his brow, deepening when Carrington did something which made maître d's heart drop.

Carrington waved his waiter over and pointed at his plate then at a table where two women… the same two for whom James had mixed cocktails… were sitting.

The young man glanced across, nodded, and then scurried into the kitchen, returning with a stack of tasting plates, then went to speak to the women who were preparing to leave.

In stunned silence, the maître d' watched the young waiter stop the pair. A brief conversation ensued, interspersed with an occasional gesture in Carrington's direction. Régis bafflement increased when he saw them nod, then weave through the other diners to Carrington's table.

Carrington rose from his seat, and helped the waiter seat the two women, moving the lobster tank to the opposite side of the table, as though it was a fourth guest.

Returning to his seat, Carrington whispered something to Adam, who blanched.

Before the maître d' could interfere, his waiter served the turkey, placing two small portions in front of the women, and the rest on other plates, which Carrington offered to whoever happened by.

The audacity, Régis thought angrily. *If you are here to critique our food, at least have the common decency to taste it. Don't make other people do your work.*

"Mr. Carrington," he addressed his wayward diner, "may I have a word with you… in private?"

Slightly taken aback by the chill in the maître d's voice, Carrington got to his feet and the two men stepped away from the table.

"Sir, I cannot condone you sharing your food with other guests. I-it's unsanitary and, I daresay, violates some health code regulation…

"My dear Régis, I promise you, the only person to apportion the turkey was your delightful waiter, Adam. I explained to anyone I offered a morsel to, my reasons for wishing to share with them. No one refused or complained, and everyone complimented the chef."

"I'll let it slide this time, sir but, if I catch you feeding them sorbet from your spoon during the next course, I will boot you out of here no matter who you work for."

"Errr… okay," Carrington replied, clearly confused. "I guarantee that will not happen."

"Really?" Régis asked skeptically.

"Yes… look."

The maître d' turned to see his waitstaff circulating through the dining room, offering customers samples of the different flavor sorbets the restaurant carried.

Some refused politely… most accepted graciously.

"Now, Régis, forgive me but, I ought to return to my guests… and if you could, please have James bring over your best bottle of Moscato. The ladies… while their taste is somewhat refined… prefer a sweet glass."

Feeling ridiculous for his outburst, and now being relegated to waitstaff, Régis shuffled to his podium, stopping long enough to relay the drink order.

James emerged from the wine cellar with a bottle clenched in each hand. Régis recognized the one carried in his left hand as a mid-level, $60 Moscato. That was fine, but the one in James' right, concerned the maître d', who questioned whether his sommelier was hiding it from him.

As James stood it on the table, Régis realized it was the 2001 Moscato, Madame Roche had purchased at auction in 2010.

With a sigh, he hustled to Carrington's table… something he was growing tired of doing.

Hooking James' arm, he pulled him back before he could plug the corkscrew into the cork, but not before the sommelier managed to remove the foil and expose it.

In James' ear, Régis whispered furiously, "Have you lost your mind? You dared to dip into Madame's private stock?"

James shrugged off Régis' grip, protesting, "Oh, please. I

doubt she even remembers it's there. Besides, with all the money this guy has been throwing around tonight, my guess is, she won't be too upset if we sell the bottle at the current market price of nine-hundred and eighty dollars; not when she has just quadrupled her investment.

"It's a stupid dessert wine for God's sake. Who wastes that much money on something that's little more than liquid candy. It's not like I chose one from her stash of 1945 Romanée-Conti Burgundy or her last bottle of 1869 Château Lafite Red Bordeaux."

"It's your head if she questions its absence," Régis warned.

"Well, we've been invited to join him to finish the bottle at close, so it is your decision as to whether you want to insult a guest.

James returned to the table, opened the Ca' d'Gal Vite Vecchia, Moscato, then collected the cheaper bottle and disappeared back into the wine cellar.

The three at the table enjoyed the effervescent wine, toasting each other and the night.

Their glasses empty, the women thanked Carrington for inviting them to his table, bade him farewell, and left.

Alone once more, he ate his way through the herb-crusted venison medallions of the second main course.

Régis glanced at his pocket watch; there was only an hour before closing.

I guess he's bound and determined to make us join him for those damned lobsters, Régis conceded.

By now, most of the patrons, after partaking of their fill, had departed. A couple of tables were occupied by stragglers, fortunate in their timing to be seated, and Carrington had moved onto the last few courses.

The cheese course featured a variety of textures and flavours; such as, aged, soft, firm, and blue, and took Carrington longer to wade through than any of the previous dishes.

While blue cheese was Régis' favourite, the same could not be said for Carrington, and the maître d' swore Carrington was forcing down every mouthful, determined not to be beaten.

The lemon crème brûlée of the penultimate course, suited the bottles of dry white wine, Carrington had consumed throughout the evening.

The diner finished his official dessert as the last of the other guests left, and Régis and lock the front door.

Munching on the chocolates, Carrington smiled as Régis joined him at the table, pouring himself a glass of overpriced Moscato.

"Looks like you have won, Mr. Carrington. I'll see the chef comes out to boil the lobsters."

"No need, I asked Adam to speak to Maurice."

"Ordering my staff around now?"

"I would never assume to take your job. Besides, I cannot pull off the French accent as well as you can, Reggie."

Reggie chuckled, "What gave me away?"

"Your pronunciation of *quoi que* was incorrect. You emphasised the wrong part. It is a common mistake we Americans make. If I was to guess, I would say New York?"

"You have a good ear."

"And the name Reggie… your parents were baseball fans?"

"That is an amazing observation, sir. May I ask how you figured that out?"

"Taking a punt on your age, I'm guessing Reggie Jackson. What New Yorker didn't name their kids after him."

"Since you're adept at reading people's secrets, your chef Maurice's name is actually Murray but, unless you're ordering a Reuben on Rye at a deli, it doesn't really fit. People expect employees of a French restaurant to have appropriate names."

There was a break in conversation as *Murray* joined them; his apron stained with the remnants of the night's orders… most of which, the result of Carrington's extraordinary meal.

Without a word, he began boiling the salted water. Once it was bubbling vigorously, he dropped the lobsters in the pot. The customary squeal denoting the water was the proper temperature.

Pulling out the third chair, the chef made himself comfortable and uncocked a bottle of Pinot Grigio. Allowing it to breathe long enough for James to join them, Murray poured himself and the sommelier a glass each, then toasted the table and drank his down in one go.

Reggie levelled a wary eye at his chef, reminding him, "That bottle better not be from Madame's private stock, cuz it's coming out of your wages."

"After the night our friend here had put us through, I think we should consider this a worthwhile tip."

Ignoring the remark, Reggie returned his attention to Carrington. "Since we are sharing secrets, would you mind me asking if you'll be giving our establishment a glowing review? I am sure Madame would appreciate it."

"I am more than happy to. Do you have compliment cards?"

"No, that's not what… wait… with the meal you ordered… aren't you a food critic?"

"Oh, good Lord, no," Carrington replied, watching the chef tend to the lobsters. "I work at the cement mill here in town."

Murray gaped at the revelation, his response mirrored by the other staff.

"B-But the cost of the meal?" Reggie stuttered.

Carrington reached into his inner coat pocket, withdrew a thick stack of bills, and handed them to Reggie. "Take what you need to cover the cost and use the rest to tip the house."

Embarrassed to do so in front of the guest, Reggie totalled the bill and subtracted it from the stack of hundreds, finding enough left for generous gratuities.

By the time Reggie had finished with the financial side of the night, Murray had cooked the pièce de résistance; the *blue* lobsters, now a vivid *red.*

With the skill of a surgeon, Murray divided up the lobsters, making sure their *host* still was served the lion's share.

Carrington raised his glass and toasted, "Thank you for joining me in this perfect farewell dinner."

His voice grew laboured, "This was more than… I ever… could… have… wished."

Busy eating the delicious sea-food, no one noticed Carrington's pallor as he forced the words out.

His eyes bulging, he slipped from his chair onto the floor.

His breathing grew ragged and shallow as the men around the table tried to revive him.

Their attempts were in vain.

The Coroner's Office

Medical Examiner, Raymond Alexander, was sitting at his desk, rereading the autopsy on one William Farnsworth Carrington. Owing to the rapid and mysterious nature of the latter's demise, Captain Zachariah Neilson, of the Bridgeton Police Department had requested a post mortem to determine cause of death.

The police captain paced Alexander's office, as was his habit. "Tell me. How does a man drop dead at a restaurant? Was it poisoning? I'll close that place down in a heartbeat if that's the case. I've never trusted the French."

"Cool your jets, Zach. If there was any malfeasance in what happened, it was self-inflicted. I'd prefer to list this as a suicide. There's no way this joker didn't know the severity of his shellfish allergy. Unfortunately, without a note affirming his intent, I have no choice but to rule it an accidental death. Death by lobster if you will." Alexander chuckled at his own wit.

Neilson jerked a cursory nod and jotted the findings in his tattered notebook. He shoved it back into his pocket, and dug out the pudgy cigar which was blocking the notebook's ease of passage. Lighting it, without bothering to ask whether the ME minded, Neilson muttered, "Then it's case closed."

"Looks like, but…"

Neilson sighed. Doc. Alexander always looked for things not obvious to anyone else. "But what?"

"I can't figure out why he squandered all that money on a meal he couldn't possibly savour."

"Why, because it was his last meal?"

"No, because there was no way he could taste it. The man had stage three brain cancer…"

"And?"

"And… given where the cancer was located, I doubt he'd been able to taste or smell *anything* for months."

The End!

Rori Bleu

With a smattering of riverboat pirates and royalty in her heritage, Rori Bleu's childhood reflected her past.
An interest in fairy tales, myth and legend were as important as spirited discussions around politics and current affairs — although some might argue they are one and the same!

A fascination, sparked by listening to Grimm's Fairy Tales at her grandmother's knee, not only encouraged Rori's passion for reading, but also steered her into the world of RPG's. What began as a fun pastime, soon evolved into the creation of fantastical worlds, but Rori never lost her love of politics going on to specialise in Governmental History and Historical Research.

Naturally this means her stories are steeped in historical accuracy and real-life intrigue. While Rori's love of a happily ever after means her preferred genre is romance, don't be surprised if you discover an occasional detour into historical fiction, thrillers, horror and fantasy.

To find more of Rori's books… click the link
https://linktr.ee/roribleu

Rosie Chapel

Rosie Chapel lives in Perth, Australia with her hubby and two furkids. When not writing, she loves catching up with friends, burying herself in a book (or three), discovering the wonders of Western Australia, or — and the best — a quiet evening at home with her husband, enjoying a glass of wine and a movie.

Website: www.rosiechapel.com

Also by Rori Bleu

Pineapple Meringue

Imprisoned Hearts

Port of London

Dani's Masquerade

Black Tulips

Ajei's Destiny

Porta Aeternum

The Queen's Heart

Syn *with Matthew Forester*

With Rosie Chapel

Echoes and Illusions

Evie's War

Vindicta

Corrupt Covenant

Lesser of Two Evils

The Sela Helsdatter Saga - with Rosie Chapel

A Flip of The Coin - Book One

Conceived Chaos - Book Two

Odin's Bane - Book Three

Valhalla's Doom - Book Four

Arcane Alchemy: Freya's Fate - *A Helsdatter Saga Novella*

The Daffodil Garden

The Unconventional Duchess

Rescuing Her Knight - *the de Wiltons:* Book One

His Fiery Hoyden

A Regency Duet

A Regency Christmas Double

Fate is Curious

A Christmas Prayer *with Ashlee Shades*

The Lady's Wager

Winning Emma

A Love Impossible

Unravelling Roana

Love Kindled

Moonbeams and Mistletoe

<u>Fairy Tale Romance</u>
Chasing Bluebells

<u>Contemporary Romances</u>
Of Ruins and Romance

All At Once It's You

Cobweb Dreams

Just One Step

His Heart's Second Sigh

<u>With Rori Bleu</u>
Evie's War

Vindicta

Corrupt Covenant

Lesser of Two Evils

Echoes & Illusions - *A Dystopian Romance*

The Sela Helsdatter Saga

A Flip of The Coin - Book One

Conceived Chaos - Book Two

Odin's Bane - Book Three

Valhalla's Doom - Book Four

Arcane Alchemy: Freya's Fate - *A Helsdatter Saga Novella*